THE MERMAID

ISBN 1 85854 204 9
© Brimax Books Ltd 1995. All rights reserved.
Published by Brimax Books Ltd, Newmarket, England CB8 7AU 1995.
Printed in France.

16612

THE MERMAID

BY

L U C Y   K I N C A I D

I L L U S T R A T E D   B Y

L Y N N E   W I L L E Y

B r i m a x   ·   N e w m a r k e t   ·   E n g l a n d

Fishing

———— • ————

Polly and Paul know where there is a stream which wanders along the edges of fields and under the trees. In some places it is hidden by overhanging grasses and bushes. The only way to tell it is there is to stop and listen for the noise it makes as it bubbles along over its stoney bed.

One day Polly and Paul were lying on the bank beside the stream trying to catch a fish. It was twisting and turning and changing direction so quickly that each time Paul thought he had it, it was gone again.

"Got it!" he shouted at last. He held up the jar.

"What kind of fish is that?" asked Polly.

"Woof!" said Billy quietly, the way dogs sometimes do.

At first glance it certainly looked like a fish. It was about the right size to be a minnow and it had a proper fish tail. But the more they looked at it, the more sure they were.

It had a little face, half hidden by streaming hair. It had arms but instead of legs, it had a fish tail.

"It's a mermaid!" said Polly. She knew perfectly well that mermaids only appeared in stories.

Billy sniffed the jar.

"Go away!" shouted a tiny, cross voice. "Go away! Don't you dare come any closer!"

Billy jumped backwards in such a hurry he bumped into Polly. She fell backwards onto the grass. Paul gulped.

The mermaid, for it really was a mermaid, reached up and caught hold of the rim of the jar. She shook her tiny fist at Paul, who was so surprised he dropped the jar.

If the mermaid had been cross before, she was crosser still when she found herself lying upside down in a puddle, with three startled faces staring down at her.

"What are you looking at?" she demanded, as she turned herself the right way up and brushed the hair away from her eyes. "Have you never seen a mermaid before?"

"Not a real one," said Polly. "I thought mermaids only appeared in books."

"They do," said the mermaid.

"Then why aren't you in a book?" said Paul.

"It is not difficult to escape from a book, you know," said the mermaid.

Billy could not resist another sniff. The mermaid hit him on the nose with her fist.

"Shouldn't you be in the water?" asked Polly anxiously. The puddle was already soaking into the ground. It would soon be gone altogether.

"And whose fault is it that I'm not?" asked the mermaid. "Pick me up and put me back where I belong!" she ordered.

Polly had no idea how to pick a mermaid up. Should she hold her by the tail so she dangled upside down? One look at the mermaid's disapproving glare told her that would be a silly idea. She made a cup with her hands and scooped her up instead.

"Stop!" shouted Paul, as Polly moved towards the stream. "If you put her back she will swim away and we will never see her again."

The mermaid squirmed and wriggled. She swished her tail and banged her fists, but still Polly managed to hold her.

What a relief it was when she was back in the jar. The mermaid scowled at them through the glass and shook her fists, but she was well and truly caught and she knew it.

"I did not escape from a book so that I could spend the rest of my days locked up in a jar," said the mermaid.

"We would like to keep you for a little while so that we can get to know you better," said Paul.

"If we let you go, will you stay in the stream so that we can come and see you?" asked Polly.

"Probably!" said the mermaid. So that is what they agreed between them.

"We'll come and see you every day," said Polly.

"Tell us your name before you go, so that we can call you," said Paul, holding the jar over the stream and almost tipping her into the water. It was a mistake, because with a flash of silver the mermaid was gone. "Did you see that?" Paul gasped.

"What a fantastic dive!" said Polly, and then she sighed a big, big sigh. "How will she know when we are here? She did not tell us her name. We won't be able to call her."

"Perhaps mermaids don't have names," said Paul. "We'll have to try something like 'coo-ee!' "

Neither of them knew, of course, whether mermaids kept the promises they made. They would have to wait until tomorrow to find out.

———— · ————

To the Rescue

———— . ————

The next morning, while everyone else was still asleep, Polly and Paul crept downstairs. They left a note on the kitchen table telling their parents they would be back in time for breakfast then they crept from the house.

The grass was still wet with dew which made their feet wet, but they didn't care. They quickly knelt down on the bank beside Billy who had run on ahead. They couldn't see anything. Neither could Billy. He sniffed about. All he could smell was waterweed and fish.

"Coo-ee . . . " called Polly softly. She waited for a reply. They could hear the water bubbling over the bed of the stream and Billy sniffing about, but nothing else.

"Coo-ee . . ." called Polly again, but nothing stirred.

"Woof!" said Billy so softly they almost didn't hear him.

"What is it?" whispered Paul, dropping down beside him. Paul and Polly held their breath and then they heard it too.

A small, cross voice was grumbling at someone.

"It's coming from over there," said Paul. They could hear the mermaid clearly now, but they still couldn't see her. "Where are you?"

"Stop asking silly questions and do something!" was the testy reply.

Paul and Polly looked at one another. What were they supposed to do? And where was she?

"Woof!" said Billy helpfully. He jumped into the stream and splashed towards a clump of waterweed.

"Will you keep still!" shouted the mermaid from somewhere in the weed.

"We're only trying to help," said Paul. He had taken his shoes and socks off and was in the water beside Billy.

Was the mermaid grumbling at them or was she grumbling at someone else? Paul looked down into the water. He could see the mermaid now. Her tail seemed to be caught in the weed.

Polly saw something Paul had missed. "There's a fish holding onto her tail," she said.

"Why is it doing that?" said Paul.

"How else am I going to pull it out?" snapped the mermaid, coming to the surface. "Stop asking silly questions and do something!"

"We need a stick," said Paul, looking all around him.

"Woof!" said Billy, which meant he understood. He splashed to the bank and went to look for one.

Paul pushed and poked with the stick. "How did everything get into such a tangle?"

"It wouldn't keep still! I kept telling it to keep still, but it wouldn't listen. It kept going round and round and the weed got tighter and tighter. If it had kept still I could have pulled it free. Now look at it!"

Paul prodded and pushed and poked with the stick. The mermaid swam round pulling out the strands as they became loose and gradually the tangle of weeds began to float apart.

At long last, with a tired flick with its own tail and a hard push from the mermaid, the fish was free. It swam away without a backward glance.

"Ungrateful thing!" grumbled the mermaid. "It might at least have said sorry for all the trouble it caused."

"At least it's free now," said Polly. "That's the main thing, thanks to you and a little help from us."

Polly and Paul sat dripping on the bank of the stream while Billy shook himself dry in the morning sun. The mermaid sat on a stone and inspected her tail for damage.

"Is it alright?" asked Polly, anxiously.

"It would have been alright a lot sooner, if you hadn't taken so long to do something," was her reply.

"We did our best," said Paul.

"Well, try to be a bit quicker next time," said the mermaid, cheekily.

"Woof!" said Billy. The mermaid splashed water over his face and then she dived off the stone and was gone.

"She still hasn't told us her name," said Polly.

"We'll have to choose one ourselves," said Paul. "Let's call her Chloe. Now let's go home for breakfast. I'm starving!"

———— • ————

Snow

———— • ————

The leaves had fallen from the trees and the days were getting colder. One morning, when Polly looked out of the window, the ground was covered in a thick white blanket.

"Paul!" called Polly. "Come and look!"

"Oh, it has snowed!" he cheered. "Let's go and build a snowman! Let's play snowballs! Let's . . . " and then he stopped.

Polly knew exactly what he was thinking because she was thinking it too. Was the mermaid alright? Was she safe or buried under a heap of snow?

They dressed quickly and hurried down to the stream to find out.

The meadow was sparkling in the sunshine. Everything looked so different. And where was the path?

"Woof!" said Billy. He knew. He led the way through the snow like a snowplough.

They almost fell into the stream, they came upon it so suddenly. It was quiet and still everywhere. The only sound was their own panting breath.

""Oh, where is she?" sobbed Polly. "Chloe . . . Chloe . . . Chloe . . . Where are you?"

"Is that stuff still falling from the sky?" asked a very irritated voice from somewhere beneath the snow. Chloe's face peered at them from under the snow that bordered the edge of the stream.

A stray snowflake drifted from the sky and came to rest on her head. It drooped round her ears like a bonnet, then slowly melted and trickled down her face.

"It keeps doing that!" she said. "It's cold and I don't like it! That's not all . . . Look at this!"

She disappeared under the bank of snow and Paul and Polly crossed to the other side of the stream so they could see where she had gone. She was sitting on a stone under a ceiling of snow. She was moving her head about as though her neck was a wobbly spring.

"Whatever is the matter?" they asked her in amazement.

"Look what happens when I stop!" she said, and stopped. A drip from the melting snow above her, fell onto her head and exploded into a shower of droplets. There is a lot of water in a drip if you are a mermaid.

"I'm not safe out there! And I'm not safe under here!" she grumbled. "I'm getting a headache, and I'm beginning to feel dizzy."

"We will build you a cave," said Paul.

Billy decided to help. Dogs are always better at digging than boys. He jumped into the water.

"Hey! What are you doing?" shouted Paul.

Billy knew what he was doing even if it didn't look like it for a while. There was mud, water and snow flying everywhere.

"Stop it! Stop it!" shouted the mermaid, turning an angry red under the brown mud which was running down her face and sticking in her hair.

Paul had mud running down his face too. He tried to grab hold of Billy's collar. But Billy wouldn't be stopped. He kept on digging until he had made a proper hole in the bank, then he stood back and wagged his tail.

"STOP IT!" shouted everyone as his tail swept water all over them.

"Woof!" said Billy, surprised by all the fuss. He scrambled onto the bank and showered them all again as he shook himself dry.

Paul realised that Billy had made a special cave for Chloe and patted him on the head, "Good boy, Billy!"

He found a large stone and put it in the cave so that Chloe would have something to sit on.

"Now you have somewhere safe and snug to stay," said Paul. "The snowflakes can't get in and even if the snow drips all day long it won't drip on you."

"Hmm," said Chloe. She sat on the stone. She made sure she had room to swish her tail without bumping it. She looked at the snowflakes falling outside. She looked at the drips falling from the snowbank. She looked out at the three faces looking in. She felt rather pleased. "It will do!"

Now they knew she was safe, Polly, Paul and Billy could enjoy the snow themselves. They played snowballs all the way home and built a giant snow-mermaid in the garden.

———— • ————

Ice and Icicles

————— · —————

The day after they made the cave for Chloe it was icy and cold. The snow was crunchy and there were icicles hanging from all the places where the snow had been dripping the day before. There was a covering of ice over the stream.

"Chloe," they called softly. "Are you there?"

"Of course I am!" she answered crossly. "How could I be anywhere else except here. I should never have listened to you!"

Chloe was glaring at them through bars of ice. She was trapped in her cave by a wall of icicles. "First it is drips and now it is these things! What are they?"

Paul explained about icicles.

"Keep well back," said Paul.

Chloe retreated to the back of her cave and Paul broke off the icicles one by one.

"It's alright. You can come out now," said Paul.

There was no answer. "Please do not sulk!" said Paul.

Polly looked into the cave. "She's not there!"

"She must be!" said Paul. "Where else can she be?" He looked in the cave but Polly was right. Chloe wasn't there!

Billy jumped on the ice and began to bark. He could see something moving under the ice.

"It's Chloe!" shouted Polly. "She's under the ice! We must get her out!"

Paul made a hole in the ice, but Chloe swam away from the hole.

"Poor Chloe!" said Polly. "She must be so frightened."

Paul quickly made another hole and then another. Soon there were holes everywhere.

"She is coming your way!" shouted Polly.

"Chloe!" they called urgently. "Chloe!"

Chloe had seen a gap in the ice. She was swimming straight towards it.

"Keep going, you're nearly there," said Paul, sighing with relief.

"Slow down!" gasped Polly as Chloe got closer and closer. They had never seen her swim so quickly. She was streaking through the water like a dart. But Chloe did not slow down. She swam straight past the hole in the ice.

"Did you see that?" asked Polly. "She was laughing!"

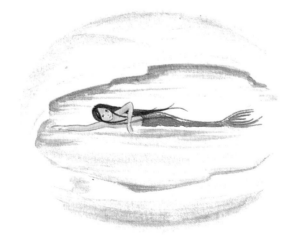

There was a giggle behind them. They turned just in time to see Chloe holding onto the ice at the edge of one of the holes. "Can't catch me!" she called, and was gone again.

"Woof!" said Billy. He chased from hole to hole, slipping, slithering and sliding. He barked and pretended to growl. And not once did he get close enough to Chloe to catch her. It was a wonderful game.

"Over here!" she would call, and then wait until Billy was almost there before disappearing with a cheeky flick of her tail. Billy got tired before she did and sat on the ice, puffing and panting.

"I knew he would not be able to catch me," laughed Chloe, popping up in the nearest hole. As quick as a flash, Billy leant forward and licked her up with his tongue.

"Don't you dare! Put me down!" shouted Chloe, hitting Billy's nose. "Put me down at once!"

Billy did not know what to do. He was as surprised as Chloe that he had caught her.

Very carefully and very gently, Paul lifted Chloe from Billy's tongue and put her back in the water. It was hard to tell who was most relieved.

"Silly dog!" said Chloe. "What did he think he was doing?"

Chloe realised that too many things had happened to her since she had escaped from the book and she did not like the ice and snow one bit. She decided to return to the book, but before she went she promised that she would return to the stream in the Spring.

"When you see the first tadpoles," she said. "Look for me. I will be there!"

———— • ————